The Fear of Angelina Domino

Story by Budge Wilson
Illustrations by Eugenie Fernandes

Stoddart
Kids
TORONTO • NEW YORK

Published in Canada in 2000 by
Stoddart Kids,
a division of Stoddart Publishing Co. Limited
34 Lesmill Road
Toronto, ON M3B 2T6
Tel (416) 445-3333 Fax (416) 445-5967
E-mail Customer.Service@ccmailgw.genpub.com

Published in the United States in 2000 by
Stoddart Kids,
a division of Stoddart Publishing Co. Limited
180 Varick Street, 9th Floor
New York, New York 10014
Toll free 1-800-805-1083
E-mail gdsinc@genpub.com

Distributed in Canada by
General Distribution Services
325 Humber College Blvd.,
Toronto, ON M9W 7C3
Tel (416) 213-1919 Fax (416) 213-1917
E-mail Customer.Service@ccmailgw.genpub.com

Distributed in the United States by
General Distribution Services
85 River Rock Drive, Suite 202
Buffalo, New York 14207
Toll free 1-800-805-1083
E-mail gdsinc@genpub.com

Canadian Cataloguing in Publication Data

Wilson, Budge
The fear of Angelina Domino

ISBN 0-7737-3217-9 (bound)   ISBN 0-7737-6120-9 (pbk.)

I. Fernandes, Eugenie, 1943–   . II. Title.

PS8595.I5813F42 2000   jC813'.54   C99-932566-3
PZ7.W54Fe 2000

*Unlike most children Angelina does not want a pet. In fact,
she's terrified of them — until just the right cat comes into her life.*

THE CANADA COUNCIL | LE CONSEIL DES ARTS
FOR THE ARTS | DU CANADA
SINCE 1957 | DEPUIS 1957

*We acknowledge for their financial support of our
publishing program the Canada Council, the Ontario Arts
Council, and the Government of Canada through the
Book Publishing Industry Development Program (BPIDP).*

Printed and bound in Hong Kong, China
by Book Art Inc., Toronto

For my friend,
Lydia Miller
— B.W.

For Julia and Noah
who have the cat
— E.F.

Angelina Domino loved animals, especially cats.
So, when she was five years old, her parents gave her a kitten.
The kitten was gray with blue eyes, and his name was Boris.

But Boris was as wild as an African lion.
He bit Angelina when she patted him.
When she picked him up, he scratched her —
every single time.
He jumped out from behind chairs
and scared the daylights out of her.

Angelina was so afraid of Boris that her
parents took him to an animal shelter,
and another family adopted him.

So, Boris was gone.

But now Angelina was scared of kittens,
and she went right on being scared,
even when Boris wasn't there.

Angelina's best friend, Josephine,
tried to help her like kittens again.
She gave her a present.
When Angelina opened it and found a toy kitten inside,
she threw the box on the floor.

"Well!" said Josephine. "I was only trying to help!"
Her feelings were hurt.

$\mathcal{M}$r. Domino took Angelina to a pet store
and pointed out all the beautiful kittens.
There were white ones and black ones
and striped ones and spotted ones.
And a gray one, just like Boris.

They had yellow eyes and green eyes and orange eyes.
And blue eyes, just like Boris.

Angelina turned her back on the cages and pretended
to look at a tank full of goldfish.

$\mathcal{M}$r. Domino showed her a gerbil running around a wheel.
"Perhaps you'd like a gerbil for a pet," he said.

"No," replied Angelina. "I wouldn't like that *at all*.
Gerbils have fur — like kittens. I bet their teeth are
as sharp as needles."

Angelina looked closely at the gerbil's feet,
keeping well away from the cage.

"Just as I thought," she said. "Claws too."

"How about a dog?" said her dad. He loved Great Danes.

"No," said Angelina. "Dogs are bigger than kittens.
They jump on you and lick you with their wet tongues.
Besides, they bark."

Then she said, "Let's go home."

One day, Angelina's mother took her to a farm.
"Cows are serious and peaceful," said Mrs. Domino.
"I'm sure you'll like cows."

Angelina hid behind her mother.
"I'm sure I *won't* like cows," she snapped.
"How could anyone like anything that big?
And listen! They snuffle and moo!
This animal is *disgusting*."

Mrs. Domino sighed.
"Then I guess you don't want to go to the zoo."

Angelina put her hands over her face.
"No *thanks!*" she cried. "Zoos have snakes. They're slithery.
And crocodiles. They're scaly. With humongous teeth.
And elephants. *Huge.* With feet that could squash you.
And very large toenails."

Mrs. Domino felt depressed.
She loved animals, even snakes.

Sometimes Josephine, Angelina's best friend, was also
her enemy. And right now her feelings were hurt.

Josephine kept chanting to Angelina:
　　"Fraidy cat! Afraid of cats!
　　Fraidy cat! Afraid of cats!"

This made Angelina very sad.

Also, mad.

One day, Josephine decided to scare Angelina.

She picked up an enormous stray cat, who was
striped like a tiger and was the color of marmalade.
Josephine marched into Angelina's house without knocking.
She went upstairs and put the cat on Angelina's bed.

After that, Josephine ran like anything,
down the stairs and out the back door.

She hid under the hedge in the backyard.
Then she waited.
She wanted to hear Angelina yell blue murder.

When Angelina came home from school, she ate an oatmeal cookie in the kitchen with her mother. Then she went upstairs.

THERE WAS THE CAT.

He was curled up in a ball, sound asleep. He was ten times bigger than a kitten. Angelina was so scared that she couldn't move or speak.

When Mrs. Domino came upstairs, she saw Angelina and the cat.

Angelina was holding her breath, and her eyes were as big as beach balls.

Mrs. Domino came over and placed her hand very softly, very carefully, on Angelina's shoulder. She wanted her to know she wasn't alone. She wanted her to feel safe.

Then her mother spoke.
"Angelina," she said. "Does that cat *really and truly* look like a fierce and dangerous animal?"

Angelina started to breathe again.
She looked at the cat.
Then she looked at him some more.
His eyes were closed and he was snoring very quietly.

"Maybe not," said Angelina.

But she came closer to her mother and hugged her leg.

"Cats are different from kittens," said Mrs. Domino.
"Often they get slow and lazy. They're usually
too busy sleeping and eating to scratch people.
They're warm and soft, and they have excellent purrs.
A purr can be a very comforting sound."

Mrs. Domino went over and lightly touched the cat's back. His eyes opened ever so slightly, and he started to purr.

"Soft," murmured Angelina's mother, as she stroked his fur.

Angelina grabbed her mother's hand and reached out to touch the cat's back.

"Soft!" she whispered. "Oh, *very* soft!"

She could feel his warm tummy rising and falling as he breathed.
She listened to his purr.

"Cat music," said Angelina.

"Yes", said her mother. "He has a wonderful song."

The cat uncurled himself and jumped down from the bed.
He yawned — wide — showing two rows of teeth.
But yawning is a whole lot different from biting.

Mrs. Domino walked over to him.
He rubbed his head against her leg.

"He's doing that," said Angelina's mother, "because he's
happy. And because he likes me. If you're *really lucky*,
he might do it to you, too."

Angelina was still scared.
She thought she might run downstairs and out the door.
She thought she might just stand in the hall and watch
from the doorway.

But she also thought she'd like to find out
if that cat liked her.

Angelina sat down on the bed, holding her breath again, but feeling almost brave. She hoped the orange cat would come up and rub against her arm.

She also hoped he would do no such thing.

Angelina began thinking some thoughts.
This is what the thoughts were:

- I hate it when dumb old Josephine calls out, "Fraidy cat! Afraid of cats!"
- I wish I could love cats again the way I used to.
- I want to take my fear and bury it in a deep hole.
- Besides, I think I kind of love this cat already.
- And I want him to like me.

- A *lot*.

Angelina cleared her throat. She coughed twice.

"Come on over, Hector," said Angelina.
"His name is Hector," she explained to her mother.

Hector left Mrs. Domino and jumped up on the bed.
Then he pressed his soft-hard head against Angelina's
arm and rubbed against it.

Oh!

Angelina's chest felt warm all over,
and full of amazement.

"He likes me a lot," she whispered.

She felt tight things inside herself becoming
loose and peaceful. She reached out her hand
and touched the top of Hector's head,
very gently, very tenderly.

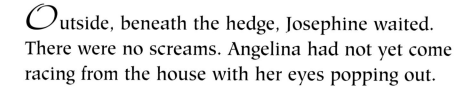

Outside, beneath the hedge, Josephine waited.
There were no screams. Angelina had not yet come
racing from the house with her eyes popping out.

Josephine was disappointed.

Then the back door opened.
Angelina came out carrying the marmalade cat.

"Get out from under the hedge, Josephine!" she yelled.
"Come see my new cat. His name is Hector.
He's old and slow and gentle.
And big, too. He doesn't scratch. He's *mine*.
Don't you wish he was yours?"

Josephine frowned.
"Yes," she said. "As a matter of fact, I do."

"Too bad," said Angelina.
"But never mind. Tomorrow we're going to the zoo.
Mommy and Daddy and me. Especially me.
Want to come?"

Josephine was too surprised to answer.

But when Angelina said, "We'll see snakes and crocodiles and elephants," Josephine was able to speak again.

"Sure," she said. "I can hardly wait!"

Josephine grinned at Angelina. She didn't feel like an enemy any more.

Hector felt just fine. After all, he had two brand new best friends.

And Angelina? Angelina felt wonderful. She couldn't think of a single thing she was scared of.